GREG AND THE CHEAT SHEETS

BY **THALIA WIGGINS**
ILLUSTRATED BY **DON TATE**

visit us at www.abdopublishing.com

Published by Magic Wagon, a division of the ABDO Group, PO Box 398166, Minneapolis, Minnesota 55439. Copyright © 2012 by Abdo Consulting Group, Inc. International copyrights reserved in all countries. All rights reserved. No part of this book may be reproduced in any form without written permission from the publisher.

Calico Chapter Books™ is a trademark and logo of Magic Wagon.

Printed in the United States of America, North Mankato, Minnesota.
102011
012012
♻ This book contains at least 10% recycled materials.

Text by Thalia Wiggins
Illustrations by Don Tate
Edited by Stephanie Hedlund and Rochelle Baltzer
Cover and interior design by Neil Klinepier

Library of Congress Cataloging-in-Publication Data

Wiggins, Thalia, 1983-
  Greg and the cheat sheets / by Thalia Wiggins ; illustrated by Don Tate.
       p. cm. -- (Making choices. The McNair cousins)
  Summary: When he skips a grade Greg finds himself in the same sixth grade class as his bullying cousin James, who would rather cheat than work hard in school.
  ISBN 978-1-61641-630-0
  1. Cheating (Education)--Juvenile fiction. 2. Honesty--Juvenile fiction. 3. Cousins--Juvenile fiction. 4. Schools--Juvenile fiction. 5. Bullying--Juvenile fiction. 6. Trinidad--Juvenile fiction. [1. Cheating--Fiction. 2. Honesty--Fiction. 3. Cousins--Fiction. 4. Schools--Fiction. 5. Bullies--Fiction.] I. Tate, Don, ill. II. Title.
  PZ7.W63856Gr 2012
  813.6--dc23
                                        2011027702

Contents

A New School Year

The first day of school found Greg running around his room gathering all of his school supplies. He snatched up folders and notebooks, trying his best to ignore that his stomach was doing somersaults.

"Hurry up, Greg," Grandpa Joe called. He and James hoisted Charles's wheelchair into the minivan. "We're going to be late."

Greg and his sister, April, lived in the Trinidad community of Washington DC. They lived with their grandparents and cousins James and Charles.

For the past few months, Greg had worked hard to help his neighbors and earn some extra money. His efforts had earned him the name Greg the Good. But now it was time for school again.

"I don't care if we're late," James muttered.

"James, be quiet," Grandpa snapped.

Finally Greg came out. He hurried in the van behind James and slammed the door shut.

"Grandpa," Greg began, buckling his seat belt, "I thought about it and I don't want to skip to the sixth grade."

"Nonsense," Grandpa said, smiling. "You're just nervous. You worked very hard last year and you were able to advance to the sixth grade. You don't think that's a good thing?"

"It is," Greg shrugged. "But I'm only eleven and the other kids will be bigger and the work will be harder."

James sucked his teeth. He was a year older than Greg but in the same class. "Don't be such a crybaby!" he told Greg. He placed his hands behind his head and leaned back on the headrest. "Besides, it's not so bad."

"Yeah, because you're repeating the sixth grade!" April called from the passenger seat. "It will probably seem like a breeze." She started to laugh. "And Greg is in your grade. It must be embarrassing to repeat a grade *and* to have your younger cousin skip and be in your classes! You must really be stupid!"

"Alright you two!" Grandpa warned.

Grandpa pulled up to the curb along the school. Then, he faced Greg.

"You'll be fine," Grandpa said. "How about you give it a week? If you still feel uncertain, we will talk with the principal about placing you in the fifth grade."

"Thanks, Grandpa," Greg said with a weak smile.

Greg hurried inside. James brushed past him and swaggered into their first class. Greg noticed a beautiful woman writing on the chalkboard. Greg read "Ms. Clemens ~ Sixth Grade History."

Ms. Clemens turned toward the class. When she saw Greg watching her, she smiled at him. Her smile made Greg feel that she was a patient, caring teacher. He smiled back and headed for a seat.

"Okay, class." Ms. Clemens raised her hand to warn the students to quiet down. "As sixth graders, you will be graduating this year. In addition, you will be taking an important nationwide test." She paced back and forth between the desks.

"That does not include what we will be covering in my class. I believe that you all can do the work." When she eyed James she tried to smile. "I hope this means you too, James."

James merely shrugged and pretended to look interested.

Greg knew James was acting, but he couldn't help but to feel sorry for James. He did his best to avoid his cousin all summer and now they were in the same class together. Greg again wondered if skipping a grade was a good idea.

"To see where everyone is in their learning, we will have a pop quiz." She walked back to her desk and picked up a small stack of papers.

"Right now?" Greg blurted. "On the first day of school!"

Several classmates murmured. Ms. Clemens continued to smile.

"Yes, Greg. Right now. In fact, we will have a series of quizzes throughout the school year."

Ms. Clemens handed several sheets of paper to each student in the front of the rows. They passed them down to the students behind them.

Greg swallowed when he received his paper. The questions seemed over his head. Ms. Clemens might as well have typed them in a different language. He sighed and got to work.

The First D

Greg was so busy thinking about the quiz after school, he didn't notice James and his friends creeping up behind him. They all took turns pushing Greg around.

"Man, I can't believe you skipped grades!" Moochie said as he pushed Greg into Troy.

"Yeah! You think you're so smart, huh?" Troy pushed Greg into James.

"Just don't think you're all that because you skipped. Don't even think about trying to help me with my homework!" James hissed in his face.

"Come to think of it, that may be a good idea," Troy chuckled. "If Greg is both the good and the smart cousin . . ."

"Then you're the bad and the dumb one!" Moochie added. "You might need Greg's help!"

James's friends laughed. Even Greg tried not to smile.

"Shut up!" James gave them all a look that made them quiet down. He pushed Greg to the ground. Before he turned to walk off, he gave Greg a look that meant trouble later at home.

The next day, Ms. Clemens handed back the graded papers. "Well done, Melissa," Ms. Clemens told a student while walking up and down the aisles.

"Mr. Rogers," she said to a boy with glasses, "you need to brush up on your Native American history."

She handed Greg his paper. She didn't say anything, but she squeezed his shoulder as she walked by. Greg frowned at the red D on his paper and sighed.

"Just as I thought," Greg muttered under his breath. "I knew I would fail this quiz!" The school bell rang. Greg joined the other students as he made his way to his next class.

Without warning, James snatched the quiz from Greg's hand. He chuckled before shoving the paper back at Greg.

James took in Greg's disappointed face. "Not so smart now, eh? Are you hoping Grandpa will let you back in the

fifth grade?" James asked with an evil smile.

Greg tried to ignore him. As he walked away he shook his head and said, "I didn't know half of that stuff!"

James heard Greg and looked incredulous. He jogged up behind Greg and said, "You're actually getting worked up about a quiz? It's only the second day of school!"

Greg turned to him. "There is a lot of pressure on me to pass. Grandpa came up to my room last night and told me how proud he was to have one of his grandchildren skip a grade."

James pushed Greg against the wall. "Don't be such a crybaby!" he hissed before he walked away.

As Greg watched James walk away, he wondered how much sleep he would get that night. He knew he would be up late studying.

Failing

"Don't worry, Greg. I'm sure you will do much better on the next one," Ms. Clemens said after she handed back his second quiz paper.

Greg frowned at another D. He groaned. James jabbed Greg hard on his shoulder. So, Greg turned to face him.

James smirked and said, "Well, you did better than me, smarty-pants!" He displayed the fat F and *See Me* Ms. Clemens had written on his quiz.

At home that afternoon, Greg started on his homework. His papers covered half of the dinner table.

"I see you're studying hard," Grandpa said when he came in. He was pinning his name tag to his security officer uniform.

"Yeah. I got two bad grades on my quizzes. I have to do better so I can pass," Greg replied.

"You'll do fine, Greg. Just work a little harder." Grandpa gave Greg a pat on the back that made him feel better.

Grandpa headed for the door. He called over his shoulder, "April is at cheerleading practice, so you and Charles have to make dinner. Grandma left out a package of pork chops. Just pop them in the oven for an hour."

"Okay, Grandpa," Greg answered.

Minutes later, Charles rolled his wheelchair into the dining room. "Did Grandpa leave yet?" he asked Greg.

Greg nodded. His face was so low, his nose almost touched the book.

"Where's James?" Charles asked.

Greg shrugged. Charles looked at Greg studying and smiled.

"I've heard that Ms. Clemens is a hard teacher," Charles said, grabbing one of Greg's books. "I had Mr. Rivers. He was easy!" Greg merely nodded.

James strode in an hour later and sat down at the dinner table. Greg barely noticed him.

"I can't believe you!" James laughed. "All of this studying because you failed a couple of quizzes? You're such a nerd!" He yanked the book from Greg's hands.

"Hey!" Greg shouted.

James stood and held the book out of Greg's reach. "Ms. Clemens is so hard. You'll never get that perfect A. So why try?"

"Because," Greg got up and jumped for the book, "I like to know that I did my best. We have to pass both Ms. Clemens's class and that nationwide test! And I couldn't disappoint Grandpa!" He finally caught the book from James. James punched Greg in the shoulder before they both sat down.

"Leave Greg alone and help me set the table," Charles said. He was having a hard time getting the pork chops out of the oven from his wheelchair.

James grabbed the pork chops and slammed them on the counter to cool. He told Greg, "I heard a boy named Sonny deals in cheat sheets."

"What?!" Greg and Charles exclaimed.

"Yeah. He's supposed to be good, too," James said with a shrug. "Almost every time he gets the correct answers to teachers' quizzes and tests. Especially if the teachers recycle old lessons, like Ms. Clemens. Moochie told me about him. Strange I never met him before . . ."

Greg gathered his books and papers into a neat pile. He looked at James and said, "I'm not going to buy cheat sheets! I'm going to study hard and whatever grade I get will be the grade I earned!"

"Suit yourself, Greg the Goofy!" James shrugged. He stuck his foot out and tripped Greg as he walked by, nearly causing the books to drop. "But Sonny is hardly ever wrong. I'm gonna take a chance on him."

Greg shook his head. When he got upstairs, he wondered how many times Sonny could get the right answers, how much he would charge, and if he would be able to memorize the answers overnight. Then he grew mad with himself. How could he even think about cheating?

The Study Group

Greg gritted his teeth when he received his next grade.

"A little better," Ms. Clemens said. She smiled weakly. Greg felt sick as his eyes fell on the D+ on the top of his paper.

"You know, Greg," Ms. Clemens bent down by his ear, "there is a study group that just started to meet. They gather in the library during lunch every other day. They go over my assignments. They're meeting today. You might want to give them a try."

"Thanks, Ms. Clemens," Greg said. He even managed a smile.

At lunchtime, Greg and his classmate, Alex, made their way to the library. There, they met several of Ms. Clemens's students.

"Man, she is one serious teacher!" Alex told the group.

"Yeah, but she makes you want to learn," a girl named Keisha said.

"She's nice, too," Greg added. Everyone agreed.

They all got to work. They divided into small groups and took turns quizzing each other. The lunch period was almost over when Greg overheard a familiar name.

"Yeah, I know Sonny. My friend bought one of his cheat sheets. It worked, too. He passed the test," Alex told Keisha.

"That's not right!" Keisha exclaimed. "He should be expelled. Why don't the teachers do anything?"

"I think the teachers suspect something. That's why Sonny never keeps the sheets on him or at school. So if they do search him, they won't find anything."

"How do you know?" Keisha asked, smiling.

"Mind your own business." Alex smiled back.

Greg pretended not to hear, but his heart raced. He wanted to meet Sonny.

That night, Greg began helping his cousins with dinner.

"I thought you were going to study," April said, handing Charles a pile of plates. "We're okay here in the kitchen."

"No worries," Greg told her. He placed silverware on the table. "I'll be up late. Besides, I think the study group will help."

James came storming in. He shoved Greg out of the way and fell into a chair at the table with a grunt.

"Nice to see you, too," April said huffily.

"Whatever." James waved his hand impatiently. "I've been looking for Sonny."

Charles shook his head. April turned to him and frowned.

"Why would you want to meet with that rotten boy?" she asked. "Decided to go into another line of work and join him?"

James burst into laughter. "No. I actually want to buy a cheat sheet from him. Ms. Clemens called Grandpa and told him about my grades. Now I have to take some desperate measures."

Both April's and Charles's mouths fell open. James laughed again.

"You better not!" April shouted. "That boy is good for nothing. Besides, what if the sheet is wrong?"

"He's never wrong." James folded his arms.

"You buy a sheet from him and I *will* tell Grandpa!" April said.

James shrugged. "Well, I guess I can't buy one if I can't find him!"

"I mean it, James!" April turned back to mashing potatoes.

"I'll go with you," Greg whispered to James.

James's eyes widened. He turned to Greg and muttered, "Well, well! What a surprise, Greg the Goofy!"

"Whatever!" Greg hissed. "I just want to meet him and see what he is all about."

James smirked and helped Greg finish setting the table.

The Trade-off

I can't believe I am doing this, Greg thought as he joined James at Moochie's door the following night. Moochie answered after the first knock.

"What's up, Rock?" Moochie and James bumped fists. James's friends had started calling him the Rock the summer before. When they all got in trouble together, they had bonded. Now the boys felt more like family to James than his own family did.

Moochie turned to glare at Greg.

"No trouble," James whispered in Moochie's ear. "He's here to meet Sonny."

"Oh." Moochie looked Greg up and down before he let him inside.

"You finally got in touch with Sonny, huh?" Moochie asked James as they sat down.

"Yeah. Turns out his brother hangs with yours," James chuckled.

"Ahh . . . birds of a feather." Moochie joined in the laughter.

Suddenly, there was a knock at the door. The boys fell silent.

"Who is it?" Moochie demanded in a low voice.

"Yo, it's Sonny!" came a low bark.

Moochie silently opened the door. A boy taller than James slithered in. He looked over his shoulder, making sure no one outside noticed. Greg eyed Sonny's black trench coat and black hat.

"Y'all ready to do this?" Sonny quickly looked over the room and the boys.

"Yeah," James said. They all sat down on Moochie's couch. Sonny pulled out a file folder from under his coat. On top was written *Ms. Clemens. Sixth Grade History.*

"You're sure that this is the next quiz?" James asked as he took the cheat sheet from Sonny.

"You want it or not?" Sonny demanded, snatching the sheet back.

"Chill." James smiled as he handed Sonny the money. "I heard you were good, but there's always the chance."

"Trust me." Sonny did not smile. He handed the paper back to James. He got up to leave and looked at Greg.

"What about you?"

Greg was tempted, but he could not help but feel disgusted with Sonny. Sonny was just another hustler doing wrong and Greg wanted no part of it.

"No, I'm good. Thanks."

"Cool." Sonny shrugged. He handed James a piece of paper.

"This is my number. Make sure you call before nine or my grandmother gets upset." He bumped James's fist before he slunk through the door.

"Man, that is one cool dude!" Moochie said, mesmerized.

"Yeah. He is so tough!" James agreed. He had a dreamy look in his eyes.

Greg looked at both of them and tried not to laugh.

Big Fat A

"James, I'm surprised!" Ms. Clemens said as she handed James his recent quiz paper. "I knew you had it in you if you put in a little effort." She squeezed his shoulder encouragingly.

James smirked as he looked at the fat A on his sheet. He glanced at Moochie, sitting two desks over. Moochie grinned back, holding up his paper, which also displayed a huge A.

James caught Greg's eye and smirked gloatingly. Greg rolled his eyes and continued to pout over the red D on his quiz paper.

I thought the study group was going to help, Greg thought. He balled the paper up and threw it in his bag. He angrily headed for the door as the bell rang.

James rammed into him hard. He put Greg into a headlock. "What'd I tell you? Sonny pulled through! I'm

going to get another cheat sheet from him tonight."

Moochie caught up to them. "Yeah, be at my house around eight."

Greg squirmed free from James's grasp. "I can't believe you two are doing this!" he hissed.

"We can!" James and Moochie said.

A Well-Earned B

That night, Greg went with James back to Moochie's.

"I knew you'd be back!" Moochie said. He smirked as he looked Greg up and down.

Greg didn't say anything. When he hesitated to enter the house, James pushed past him into the living room.

Sonny sat on a couch, playing Moochie's video game on the big screen TV. Moochie joined him and resumed playing.

"So you in, Greg?" Sonny asked without taking his eyes off of the screen.

"Um . . ." Greg mumbled. His throat felt dry. He looked at James, who nodded. "I guess so."

"Cool. It's ten dollars per sheet. Ms. Clemens's next quiz is a tough one, but I have all the right answers," Sonny said. "Now, where's your money?"

After they paid Sonny, Greg walked back home in silence beside his cousin. The folded paper in the back of his pants felt like fire against his leg.

"I'm proud of you, Greg," James said as he put his arm around his cousin.

Greg shrugged his arm off. "Proud of me?! Whatever! I know cheating is wrong, but I want to do well."

"Well, you will. So, how does it feel to cross from good to bad?" James sniggered.

Greg didn't answer. He felt ashamed of himself for buying the cheat sheet. But, he ignored the bad feeling.

Later, Greg tried to make himself memorize the cheat sheet. He glanced over at his school books. His cheeks still burned with humiliation when he thought about James knowing he was cheating.

He looked at the cheat sheet again. "I can't do this!" he exclaimed. Then he grabbed his school books and opened them.

"I am going to study the right way. The cheat sheet is only a precaution."

"Great improvement, Greg!" said Ms. Clemens two days later. She hugged him after she handed him the quiz paper. His jaw dropped at the big B on his paper.

Greg smiled and then frowned. He wondered if he did well because he studied, or because of the cheat sheet.

James shouted, "Congrats, man! Nice to see you've improved!" He slapped Greg's back really hard. Several students laughed.

"James!" Ms. Clemens exclaimed. "Not so hard, please. I know you're as happy as I am that Greg is improving."

Greg's cheeks burned with anger. He wanted to say something, but he didn't want Ms. Clemens to overhear.

Later that night, he and James stopped at Moochie's house. Greg didn't like cheating, but he wanted to pass and make Grandpa Joe proud.

Such a Dummy

Greg sat at the dining room table memorizing his cheat sheet. He felt James watching him. He finally grew angry and put the cheat sheet in his bag.

"This is the last one," Greg told James. James merely smiled. Greg ignored him and helped himself to the dinner cooling on the stove.

"You said that last time," James reminded Greg.

"Cheating is wrong!" Greg declared. He turned to James and continued, "Besides, we are just fooling ourselves.

If we don't know this stuff, how will we pass the final exam?"

"Sonny will probably have the answers to that, too." James shrugged.

"What if Sonny gets caught?"

"You worry too much," James said, shoving collards into his mouth.

"Okay," Greg continued, "what about next year? The teacher will assume that we know this stuff, so next year will be harder and we will have to cheat again and again!"

"Luckily, Sonny knows the teachers at the junior high school! He'll be rich before we graduate!" James joked.

"That's not funny." Greg shook his head. He slammed his plate on the table. Then he reached into his book bag and pulled out the cheat sheet. He ripped it into shreds.

"What are you doing?" James shouted in disbelief. He dropped his fork.

"I can't depend on Sonny for the rest of my life! I've got to depend on myself! If I cheat, I'm only cheating myself!" He turned to James.

"I'm going to my room to study. You're welcome to join me," Greg announced. "Tomorrow I am going back to the study group. I'm going to do my best and pass the sixth grade the right way!"

James rolled his eyes. "You're making a big mistake. You know Ms. Clemens is hard. It'll be a miracle if you pass!"

"If I don't then I will study harder next year!" Greg headed up the stairs.

"You're such a dummy! And I thought you were smart!" James yelled. "You'll regret this!"

Greg ignored him and kept climbing.

A Cheat Is Caught

"I have some important news, class," Ms. Clemens announced. She stood in front of her class looking very serious. "I have received word that a young man named Sonny has been selling cheat sheets of my old lesson plans. So, I have decided to change my lessons around.

"Since I have no proof, I won't accuse anyone of buying the cheat sheets," she said.

Greg could tell she was trying her best not to look at both James and Moochie. He was terrified that she might even look his way!

Ms. Clemens continued, "However, you can all be assured that cheating will not be tolerated at this school. Sonny is not only suspended but facing expulsion."

Greg heard a small gasp from beside him. He knew it was James.

"I will be stepping up my lessons," Ms. Clemens said. "I hope many of you can keep up. We still have work to do. Don't forget that there is a study group that meets every other day in the library at lunchtime." With that, she began handing out new exam papers.

Greg looked over his paper. He looked it over again. He knew the answers!

I can do this, he thought, *I studied and I know the answers!*

Greg was so excited that he finished the exam before the rest of the class. Quietly, he walked to Ms. Clemens's desk to hand it in.

"I could grade it now if you like," she said as she took the paper from him.

Greg managed a smile and nodded. The answers were still dancing in his head.

"You know, Greg," Ms. Clemens began, lowering her voice, "I heard a lot of great things about you. I heard you have worked hard in school and in your neighborhood." Then she tapped his exam paper. "I see the study group has helped."

Greg chuckled nervously. "I've been studying at home, too," he whispered. He ignored the shame he felt for cheating.

"Well, if you continue working hard in school and doing the good things you do in the neighborhood, you can do anything you want in the world. If you need help, let me know." She handed back his paper. "Say hello to your grandfather for me."

"Thanks, I will," Greg said as his classmates started bringing their papers to her desk.

Just then, the bell rang. As he gathered his books and headed to the hall for his next class, Greg thought about what Ms. Clemens said. He felt proud of his decision to no longer cheat.

In the hall, Greg caught up with James on the way to their next class.

"You should come to the study group," Greg told James quietly. "You don't have to fail."

James looked like he wanted to hit him. "I am not going to study with a bunch of nerds! If I ever get my hands on that Sonny . . ."

"Suit yourself," Greg said, placing his exam paper in his folder. A red B sat at the top.

New Study Group

"I am very grateful that you were all here to help me," Greg told the study group. "With your help, I'm getting better grades and will be able to pass Ms. Clemens's class!"

"Me too," Alex said.

"Are we going to study or act like a bunch of girls?" James cut in, opening his book.

"Yeah!" Moochie joined in. He looked at his book as if he had never seen it before.

Greg smiled. He opened his book and glanced at his cousin.

"James, what's the answer to number seven?" Greg asked.

James looked hard at the study question then closed his eyes.

"Um . . . C," James said.

Everyone cheered.

"Whatever." James looked both angry and pleased with himself.

Just then, the end-of-lunch bell rang. Everyone gathered their belongings and headed for their next class.

In the hall, Troy and a small group of boys were looking for James and Moochie. Troy's eyes widened when he saw his friends leaving the library with Greg and the study group.

"So I guess Greg *is* giving y'all lessons!" Troy joked. He and the boys laughed.

James grabbed him by the collar. Everyone stopped laughing. Troy looked scared.

"No more jokes!" James said calmly. "Maybe Greg could help you with your spelling! Even I know you don't spell *pitiful* with two p's!"

Everyone laughed except Greg and Alex. James looked at Greg and winked, then he let Troy go. James put his arm around his cousin and together they made their way to their next lesson.

At the end of the quarter, everyone was looking forward to a break. The

McNair family was having a cookout to celebrate everyone's report cards.

"So, Greg, is your school year all that bad?" Grandma Rose asked. She handed April a plate of ribs to pass down to James.

"It is challenging," Greg admitted. "But I learned that hard work will pay off in the end."

James rolled his eyes. Grandpa noticed.

"You weren't so stuck up when you saw that C on your report card, James," Grandpa said. "I've never seen such a big smile on your face! And I hope you continue that extra effort."

James rolled his eyes and shrugged. He caught Greg smiling at him. He smiled back and kicked him under the table.

The End

Making Choices
Greg the Good

Every decision a person makes has a consequence. Greg the Good made some good and some bad decisions. Let's take a look:

Decision: Greg chose to buy a cheat sheet from Sonny.

Consequence: Greg knew cheating was wrong, and he felt ashamed.

Decision: Greg chose to stop cheating and study hard on his own and with the study group.

Consequence: Greg was proud that his hard work earned him a good grade.

Making Choices
James the Rock

Every decision has a consequence. James the Rock made some good and bad decisions. Let's take a look:

Decision: James chose to cheat to get a passing grade.

Consequence: Ms. Clemens suspected James of cheating and watched him more closely.

Decision: James and Moochie joined Greg's study group when Sonny was suspended.

Consequence: James earned his best grade yet and made himself and his family proud.

About the Author

Thalia Wiggins is a first-time author of children's books. She lives in Washington DC and enjoys imagining all of the choices Greg and James can make.

About the Illustrator

Don Tate is an award-winning illustrator and author of more than 40 books for children, including *Black All Around!*; *She Loved Baseball: The Effa Manley Story*; *It Jes' Happened: When Bill Traylor Started to Draw*; and *Duke Ellington's Nutcracker Suite*. Don lives in the Live Music Capitol of the World, Austin, Texas, with his wife and son.